WHAT'S CLAUDE DOING?

FOR MARJORIE NAUGHTON

Clarion Books
Ticknor & Fields, a Houghton Mifflin Company

Library of Congress Cataloging in Publication Data
Gackenbach, Dick.
What's Claude doing?
Summmary: A dog refuses all the neighborhood pets'
invitations to come out to play, not admitting that
he's generously keeping his sick master company.
[1. Dogs—Fiction   2. Friendship—Fiction]   I. Title.
PZ7.G117Wh 1984   [E]   83-14983
ISBN 0-89919-224-6

Printed in the U.S.A.
Y 10 9 8 7 6 5 4 3 2 1

WHAT'S CLAUDE DOING?

DICK GACKENBACH

CLARION BOOKS / TICKNOR & FIELDS / NEW YORK

"Hey, Claude!" Bruno and Mikey called out. "Come to town with us. The butcher is giving away bones."

"I'm sorry," said Claude. "But you'll have to go to the butcher without me. I can't go today."

"These are great bones," said Mikey with his mouth full.

"You bet!" said Bruno. "Too bad Claude isn't here to enjoy one."

"Come on out, Claude," shouted Jackson and Honey. "The school bus is coming!"

"I wish I could," answered Claude. "But I can't go today."

"Meeting the school bus is the best time of the day," said Honey.

"It sure is!" Jackson agreed. "Claude is missing all the fun."

"Yo, Claude!" called Bebe and Lottie. "The kids have gone ice skating. Let's go join them."

"Sorry," said Claude. "Not today!"

"WHEE-E-E!" said Bebe as she slid across the ice.

Lottie fell down on her tail. "It's a shame Claude isn't here," she said. "He loves the frozen pond."

"Claude can't catch us!" cried Pussywillow and Fang. "Come out and chase us up a tree, Claude."

"I can't chase you today," said Claude.
"I'm busy!"

"It's no fun to climb a tree by ourselves," Pussywillow said to Fang.

"No," said Fang. "It's no fun without Claude."

"What's Claude doing?" all the animals wondered.

"Ah-choo! Ah-choo!" sneezed Sam. "Thanks for keeping me company," he said to Claude, his dog. "Without you, it would have been a very lonely day."

"Good night, old pal. AH-CHOO!"